A Very Important Trip

Darryl Busink

A Very Important Trip
Copyright © 2022 by Darryl Busink

All rights reserved. No part of this publication may be reproduced, distributed, or transmitted in any form or by any means, including photocopying, recording, or other electronic or mechanical methods, without the prior written permission of the author, except in the case of brief quotations embodied in critical reviews and certain other non-commercial uses permitted by copyright law.

Tellwell Talent
www.tellwell.ca

ISBN
978-0-2288-5585-9 (Hardcover)
978-0-2288-5584-2 (Paperback)

This book is dedicated to my children, Elizabeth and Daniel, the real inspiration for this story.

Elizabeth and Daniel had just gotten off the phone with their cousins in Taiwan. Elizabeth asked, "Mama, when can we visit them again? It's been a long time".

"We don't know honey. Traveling across the ocean is very expensive for a family of four. When we have the money, we'll go back." Then their Dad said, "You know, you can actually get there by boat right from our very own back yard".

They didn't believe their dad, so they called their grandpa just to make sure. He said, "Your dad's right, but it would take a very long time and could be dangerous."

Then their grandma took the screen. "You'd also need food and water. One's body has to stay strong, or you could never make it. You can't just eat fish every day."

That night, after their parents were in bed, Elizabeth and Daniel went to the back shed and pulled out their father's rowboat. They put the paddles in and dragged it to the shore.

They knew they would face some troubles along the way, so they brought with them their bow and arrows, five chocolate gold coins, 4 sticks of bubble gum, and a few other important things. They also took one of their cats and left the other for their parents, to keep them company.

Lastly, they grabbed a beach bucket filled with fruit, two milk jugs filled with water, a shower curtain, and the sheet and blanket from Daniel's bed. After leaving a note for their parents, they shoved off into the river and were on their way.

Early the next day their parents saw a message on the fridge. It said, "Mom and dad, we are using the rowboat to go see Ama and our cousins in Taiwan. We'll call you when we get there. Don't worry, we brought supplies. Love you lots."

"What?!" their mother cried. "How could they do this to us?! They'll never make it!"
"Oh, I don't know, honey," their father replied. "They're pretty smart kids. And it was very thoughtful to leave us a note."

By sunrise, the river had taken them to a bigger river, and by midday they had reached the ocean. "Are we close to Taiwan yet?" Daniel asked his sister.
"Not yet," she replied. "It will take a long time."

Daniel realized that while many boats were passing by, theirs was almost standing still. "We need a sail," he told his sister. She pulled down the bedsheet, tied the ends to the pole, and the boat instantly started picking up speed.

At night they lay down next to each other under Daniel's blanket, with the cat curled up between them. When they were thirsty, they drank from a jug and let the cat drink from a pool formed by their cupped hands.

After two days at sea, Daniel was hungry and wanted to eat a gold coin. "No, Daniel," his sister said. "We might need it for later." Elizabeth peeled a banana and gave half of it to her brother.

Not two hours later, Daniel called out, "Look, a pirate ship!" Elizabeth wasn't sure that pirates were in fact real, but was prepared just in case. "You're right!" she said, "and I think they're coming closer!"

In no time, the ship had pulled in the rowboat and a plank was set out. The captain followed. "Ahoy mateys," he hollered. "You be travelin' alone on this mighty sea? We be searchin' fer gold. If ya give us some, we'll leave ya alone."

Elizabeth opened her sachet and revealed the 5 coins. The captain saw them immediately and yelled out, "Arrr, give them to me, missy, and another day yee shall see."

She handed the sachet to her brother, who said, "Um, Elizabeth, these are –".
"The rarest gold coins that you ever will see," she interrupted. Grabbing them from her brother, she threw them to the captain, and said, "Now please, just let us be."
Pulling one to his nose, the captain said, "These coins indeed, are a different kind of breed. Why, they be givin' me hunger, instead of wanting to plunder." And with that, his men retrieved their plank and went on their way.

Daniel's hunger continued, and he grew tired of eating fruit. "I wish we had a fishing rod," he told his sister. "I see lots of fish. If only we could catch one."

Elizabeth pulled out the bow and arrows and began ripping off the suction cups. She reached in her pocket and took out three small nails and stuck them in each arrow where the suction cup was. She then tied a string to the first arrow.

Standing at the back of the boat, she took aim at the nearest swimming fish and released the arrow. "Aw, you missed," Daniel stated. He pulled the string and grabbed the floating arrow.

Elizabeth grabbed the arrow again, waited longer this time, and tried again. "You got it! You got it!" Daniel screamed in excitement. "Good shooting! Let me try next time!"

As quick as lightning, the cat came jumping up to see the fish, and began pawing away at the flapping tail. Elizabeth smiled and said to the cat, "We can eat again."

After a few more days, the waves became violent and began to crash onto the little rowboat. "I'm scared!" Daniel yelled.
"Here, the shower curtain," Elizabeth yelled. "Get everything under it!"

The storm was big and the boat swayed up and down like a roller coaster. Water began filling up the boat and Elizabeth noticed some tiny cracks in the hull. "Where's the gum?" she shouted. Daniel found it and looked at her.

"Let's chew it, quick!" she said. After a minute, she removed it from her mouth and placed it on the crack nearest to her. "You do the same!" She then grabbed the bucket and began emptying the boat of water.

Days went by and the siblings passed the time by singing songs they had heard from their parents, playing card games, and guessing what their parents were eating for dinner that day.

One day, they woke up and found that their row boat had reached land. An old man asked them where they came from. "Really far away," Elizabeth replied. "We came to see our Ama and cousins."

The old man took them to a taxi. "You are very brave," he said. "Where do they live?"
Daniel took out a piece of paper. "We have their phone number."

Standing at the door was their Ama, Uncle, Aunt, and their three cousin
"You made it!" Ama shouted, and gave them a hug. "Someone's be
missing you," she said, and handed Elizabeth a phone.
"Hi Mama. Hi Daddy. We love you!"

CPSIA information can be obtained
at www.ICGtesting.com
Printed in the USA
LVHW072303150622
721366LV00002B/8